SARDINE
in outer space
5

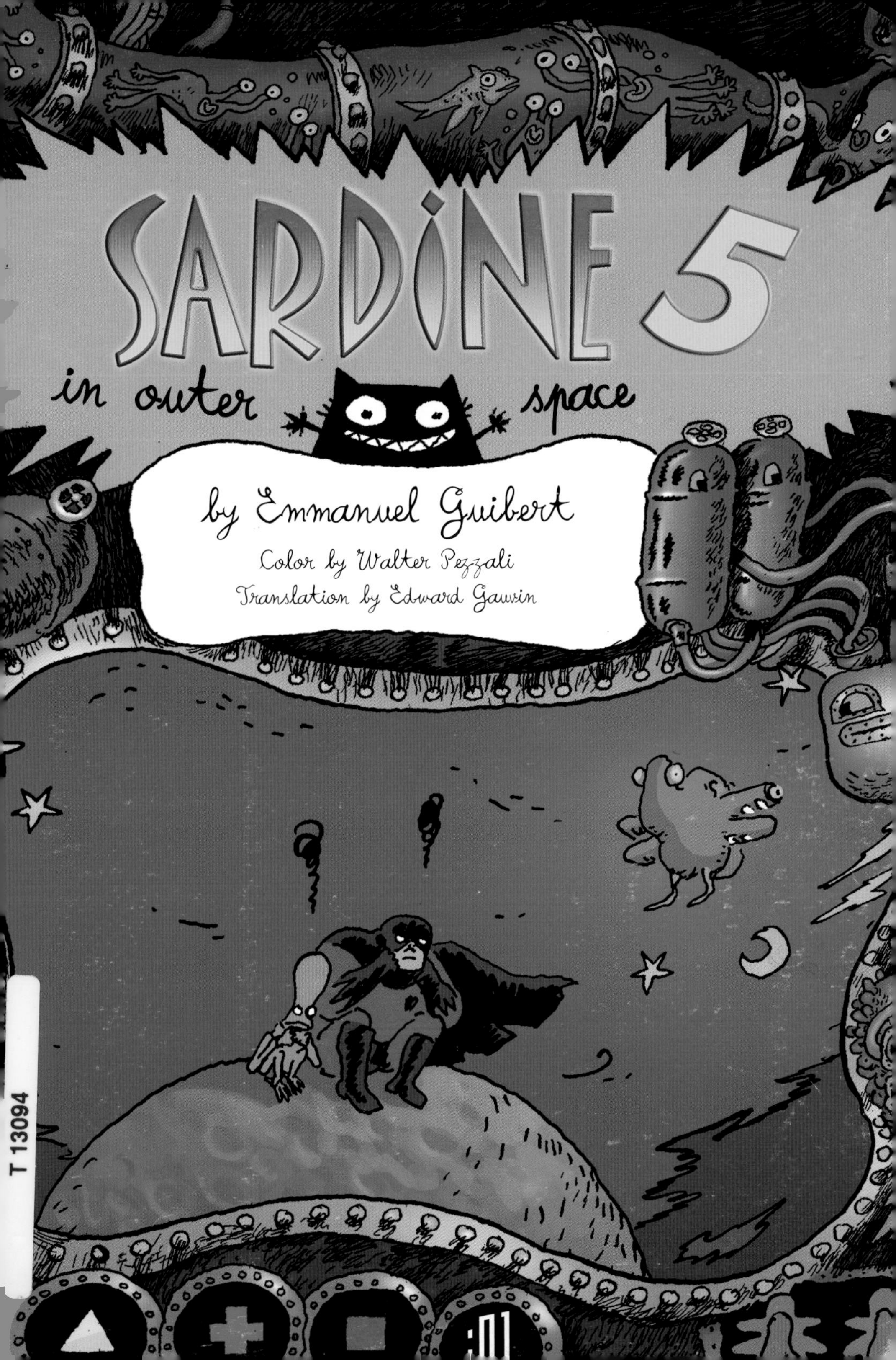
SARDINE 5
in outer space
by Emmanuel Guibert
Color by Walter Pezzali
Translation by Edward Gauvin

Contents

The Bold and the Bashful
Where are we, Uncle? It's really dark here.
We're on the dark side of the moon, Sardine. I've heard that people live here. I'd like to know what they look like.
Let's go ask that guy over there.
SMOOCHIE

Hey, Mister!
AAAH!
G-go away, p-please! D-don't talk to me!
No need to be afraid!
We won't hurt you!
L-leave me alone! Don't talk to me, or look at me, or touch me!
Why? Are you sick?
No – worse!
I'm shy!
I'm the president of Shyovia – the Republic of the Bashful!

Where are your fellow citizens?
They're all hiding in their houses, afraid to come out! And I was supposed to give a speech today ...
Is that why you're up on a podium?
Yes, but no one's come to hear me, because Shyovians hate public assemblies.
It's just as well, since I'm terrible at public speaking.
Say, it must be weird being president when you're shy.
It's dreadful! I'd love to change jobs, but no one will swap with me. You don't want to, do you?
No, not us! We're not Shyovians!

And I haven't even told you the worst part! I'm in love!
That's great, Mr. President!
Congratulations!
clap clap
No, it's so saaaaad! Our love is dooomed! The woman of my dreams is the Sunnysiders' president!
The Sunnysiders? Who are they?
The Sunnysiders live on the other side of the moon, the sunny side. They're light-hearted and party all the time. The opposite of us Shyovians!
A poor Shyovian would never have the courage to go and declare his love to a Sunnysider!
So we'll go for you instead!

Soon, on the other side of the moon ...
We definitely have to rescue that poor president from his dark thoughts.
There's Sunnyside's presidential mansion.
POW!
BOOM!
POP!
POW!
ALWAYS OPEN
VISITORS WELCOME
Everyone's partying and laughing.
Hey! You guys! C'mere!
I'm the security chief, and I've got orders to let everyone in. Champagne?
Sure, but most of all we'd like to meet your president.

Well, my darlings? I heard you wanted to see me!
Yes, Madame President. We represent the president of Shyovia.
HA HA HA
Hee hee
Ick!
He's in love with you, but he's afraid to let you know.
He's too shy!
He's all alone, crying in the dark!
BLAH BLAH
HO HO
The poor darling! Well if he's afraid to come out, I'll just go find him! That way I can see what he looks like.
Bravo!
YEAH
HEE HEE
Darling, I'm leaving with these three on official business. Keep partying while I'm gone. I'll be back soon.
Yes, President.
YIPPIE
CHEERS

Back in the shadows ...
President, we brought you Madame President.
Well, darling! I heard you were afraid to come see me?
NOOOO! Don't come any closer! Don't touch me! Don't talk to me!
Ha ha! How funny, being back in Shyovia!
What? You, a Sunnysider, have been to Shyovia?
?
Of course I have! I used to be a Shyovian!
N-no kidding?

How do you go from being a Shyovian to a Sunnysider?
By taking a nice warm sunbath!
B-but I'd have to wear a bathing suit in public! I'd never have the nerve!
No nerve needed, darling! I'll take care of it.
NOOO! Let me go! I'll die of shame!
Later, in Sunnyside again ...
Well, darling? Don't you feel better now?
No – I mean, yes ...
TICKLE TICKLE
Ha ha! The president's true colors are shining through!

A little birdie said you were in love with me. Was that tiny tale true?
No ... I mean, yes ...
It's true! I'm crazy for you! Marry me, sweetheart, and we'll make our countries one!
Hooray!
Thank you, Yellow Shoulder, Sardine, and L'il Louie! I feel like a new man.
Much obliged, darlings.
Heh ...
SMACK
Look at Uncle: he's shy as a Shyovian!
HA HA

We should give a speech, telling our two countries the good news!
Let's do it on TV. That way the Shyovians at home will see it too.
Soon, on every screen on the moon ...
Shyovians, Shyovians! Stop being so nega-tive! Get out of your houses and into the light! You'll grow truly sunny!
Sunnysiders, Sunnysiders, my darlings! Let's leave our sunny land to our friends the Shyovians and try out the shade. We'll party all night for twice the fun!
All they have to do now is mix and mingle!
CORN HORNS
The End

The Scamcorder
Supermuscleman! I've found a new way of making children's lives miserable!
Are you going to film me, Doc Krok?
HANDLE
SMM

Listen up and I'll explain! This is no ordinary camera. It's the SCAMCORDER!
Go ahead, shoot me while I'm doing push-ups!
nine ten eleven twelve
Watch carefully. I'm going to shoot this pig. Aaand-action!
But why shoot a pig when you can shoot me?
thirteen fifteen eight-een
WHIR-RR
HAHA! Look! He's breaking out in zits all over!
?
WHRRR
OINK?
That's disgusting!
Now, to up the power, I zoom in!
BZZOOOO

... and he's covered in hair!
That's better. It hides the zits a little.
BNNOOOO.
OIIINK!
For the finale, I zoom out.
Does that make feathers grow?
BZEEEEE
No! It makes his ears grow! HAHAHA!
Heh, heh- funny! My turn now!
EEK! EEK! EEK!
Go ahead, Doc Krok! Shoot me doing push-ups.
Have you heard a thing I said, Supermuscleman?!

The Scamcorder isn't really a camera! It's a weapon!
Really? What for?
These days every parent in the universe has a camcorder to film their kids. Well, we'll sell them Scamcorders instead!
The Scamcorder doesn't shoot film. It shoots a ray that makes you pimply, hairy, and big-eared!
There's even a button for buckteeth.
pimples
ears
hair
teeth
nose
That way, every kid in the universe will be as ugly as that pig!
HAHAHAHAHA! Serves them right!

Soon, aboard a vessel not unfamiliar to us ...
We've had it, Uncle! You never take pictures of us!
Yeah! When we're big, we won't be able to see what we looked like when we were little!
Just reread the comics.
It's not the same! Drawings are nice, but photos are really real.
And I look better in photos.
Okay, fine. I'll buy a camera. A cheap one, y'hear?
HOORAY!

Let's go to Planet F-Stop. That's where all the photo stores are.
Look who's coming, Supermuscleman! It's that dratted Yellow Shoulder in his ship, the Huckleberry!
Let's find a cannon to fire at him!
SUPER M
PHOTO SHO
Now on sale: SCAMCORDER
No, I've got a better idea! We'll slip him the Scamcorder! Quick, let's disguise ourselves.
As what?
SUPER M
STOCK
I've got everything planned! Here, put on this Scamcorder salesgirl outfit.
Okay!
Red-Eye Pen For Your Polaroids
FILM
ISO 100
ISO 200
ISO 400
AUNTIE

Hello, ladies.
Hello, Yell-OW!
HEL-lo sir! Hi, kiddies! Come in, come in!
If you have blackheads on your nose, ask for our ENLARMENTS 50 blackheads= 1 free enlargement
SUPER
STOCK
LEIKON
Pay for your mistakes: botched photos are TWICE the price
Your photos in just 1 hour (but ugly)
I'm looking for a basic camera – cheapest thing you've got.
I've got something much better: the Scamcorder!
The amazing Scamcorder just hit stores. There's a ten-year free trial period. Instead of tired old still photos, you'll get real live action that walks and talks.
That's it, Uncle!
Let's get that one!
ARM ADILLO

Can I try it out, just to see?
NO WAY!
NO, NO!
You can use it on Sard –
OW!
With your lovely children. The instructions are very simple. Here, take them.
PHOTO CONTEST
Look here
Press here
Well, Sardine? L'il Louie? Happy now?
Very happy!
SCAMCORDER
We'll goof around, and you can record us!
No, I have a better idea. Let me borrow the Scamcorder, Uncle.
?

What're you gonna do?
Did you see that big-eared, hairy animal in the store?
Yeah.
It's funny looking. Let's get it on tape before we go.
Look, it's between the two salesladies. Action!
WHIRR
..click
Can I take my costume off, Doc Krok? It itches.
AAAH!
You're b-b-breaking out all over!
SCRITCH
SCRATCH
SCRITCH
SCRATCH
SCRATCH
You're covered in pimples too!!
And y-you're covered in HAAAIR!

Hey, Sardine! Aren't those two salesladies Supermuscleman and Doc Krok?
I think so. But they've got great disguises.
AAAAAH
AAAAAH
WHIRR
Later ...
Hey, Sardine! Film me, I'm the winner!
Better not, L'il Louie. This Scamcorder's a total scam.
OWK! OWK! OWK!
I found a real camera. Now I can take a good old-fasioned photograph!
GRRRR
GRRR
Thbbbt!
The End

Skoolmaster
Hey Uncle, can you find us a schoolmaster?
Or a schoolmistress?
You kids wanna go to school?
CAUTION
THAT MEANS YOU
TATTOOEY

Not really, we just want to have summer vacation.
Whatcha mean, summer vacation?
Since we never have school, we never have summer vacation. See?
I've heard summer vacation is awesome!
Okay. At any rate, it wouldn't hurt you to study some.
Yeah, but only easy things!
Things we know already!
Let's look on the Galaxy-web. I'll post: Skoolmistress.
It wouldn't hurt you to study some either, Uncle.

Later.
DING DONG
The door!
It must be the schoolmistress!
I'll get it.
Greetings, comma, is this the residence of Captain Yellow Shoulder, question mark?
Uh – yes. Are you the – uh, teacher?
HUCKLEBERRY
80
Indeed, period. Lead me to my students immediately, exclamation point!
80
HEY EVERYBODY! The schoolmaster's here!
But we asked for a schoolmistress!
Yeah!
HAHA HA!
Yippee!

SILENCE exclamation point!
Welcome aboard the Huckleberry, Teach.
I take it you are Captain Yellow Shoulder, question mark?
Yep, that's me.
Well, comma, it's nothing to be proud of, exclamation point! Not only are your brats ill-bred, comma, but you spell like a slob, period.
M-me?
Your ad on the Galaxyweb was riddled with errors, exclamation point! Go stand in the corner, period.
Off to a great start!

Shape up, comma, children, period. Have you a blackboard, question mark?
No, comma, we're one black-board short ...
... period!
But there's a black hole out there!
I care not for your black holes, exclamation point! I shall use Squeaky, period.
What's Squeaky?
My special chalk, comma, see, question mark?
squeak
squeak
OOH!
It writes in midair!
It writes on air!
Yeah!
HAHA HA!
clap
clap

Can you tell me what letter I've just written, question mark?
Easy, that's a "p"!
a
Captain, comma, I don't recall calling on you, period. Worse yet, you've spoken up with the wrong answer, exclamation point!
It's not a "p"?
Heeheehee!
Put this dunce cap on, comma, face the wall, comma, and don't interrupt any more, period.
DUNCE
Pfft! I've had enough!
Psst – L'il Louie? Y'know why Uncle didn't get an "A"?
Nope.
Because he took a "p"!
HAHAHA!
Hee Hee

YOU TWO, exclamation point! Go cool your heels in space – you need to settle down, period.
We didn't do anything, sir!
C'mon, L'il Louie, let's get outta here ...
See you later, Uncle!
We're not doing too well, kids ...
DUNCE
See here, comma, where has my chalk Squeaky gone, question mark?
Well, comma, it matters not, period. I have another, period.
To continue, dot dot dot ...

A little later ...
The children should be calmer by now, period. I shall tell them to come back in, period.
WARNING: DOOR to OUTER SPACE
80
BOOM
80
I found these two whippersnappers writing mean slogans about me in outer space!
HANDS UP EVERY-ONE! School's out!
GRRR
hee hee
80

DUNCE
Huh?
POW
POW
Yay, Uncle – you're the best!
Yeah!
Captain, comma, I owe you so many thanks, comma, you'll get a star, period.
Star, heehee!
Krok and Supermus-cleman saw stars!
I'm sorry I punished you, comma, Captain, period.
Don't be sorry. If you hadn't put me in the corner, I couldn't have surprised those two morons.
Here's your chalk back, sir.

soopermuscleman is a big ignoramus
We used it to write in outer space a little.
I see, exclamation point! Let's correct this lovely sentence together, dot dot dot ...
When's summer vacation?
The End period.

Pilot-o-Matic
Why'd you leave the Huckleberry in the garage, Uncle?
Because it needs a good tune-up.
What are we gonna do without it? We're supposed to eat at Grandma's tonight.
GARAGE
MOEBIUS BROS

We'll do what everyone without a spaceship does and take public transportation.
COOL!
ASTROPORT
There's the Astroport. Let's get our rocket tickets.
ASTROPORT
ASTROHALL 1
SPACE TAXI
scribble
DING DONG
Flight 29664 to Pluto has been delayed.
DANG DING
A young green gentleman with 5 tentacles and 3 trunks is waiting for his parents at Counter 20.
DONG DANG
duty-fresh
dentipaste
Air Space
planet flight
MARS 4
A2814 TAU CETI 1
A2814 MOON 8
It's huge!
All aboard for Jupiter, Gate 7.

Hello, I'd like 40 tickets, please – 39 children's fares.
That'll be 1,000 aeros.
STRATOS AIR
Expensive, huh, Uncle?
Yeah. Good thing Grandma's helping us pay for it.
Heh heh ...
They've sure got some surprises in store for them!
HAHAHAHA!
Take off!
With Stratos Air
Jupiter-Mars in 3 hours!
STRATOS AIR
Soon ...
C'mon! Everyone on board!
CLAP CLAP
STRATOS AIR

Hello, greetings, welcome aboard!
Hi, Ma'am.
Hm. That's odd.
You look like the lady who sold us our tickets at the astroport.
HA HA yes! Naturally, she's – my brother!
Her brother? Something fishy's going on ...
Let's grab our seats, kids.
Dibs on porthole!
Everyone's on board, Supermuscleman.
Perfect! What they don't know is that they're not headed for Grandma's ...
They're heading straight to jail!
HOHOHOHOHO!
HAHAHA!
KA-THOOM

Uncle, since I haven't stopped drinking soda all episode, I'm going to the bathroom, okay?
Okay, but be quick.
I will now demonstrate a few safety measures. Please listen carefully.
Boy, that steward-ess is ugly.
Hush, L'il Louie! This is important.
In case of sudden loss of cabin pressure, a red nose like this one will automatically drop in front of you.

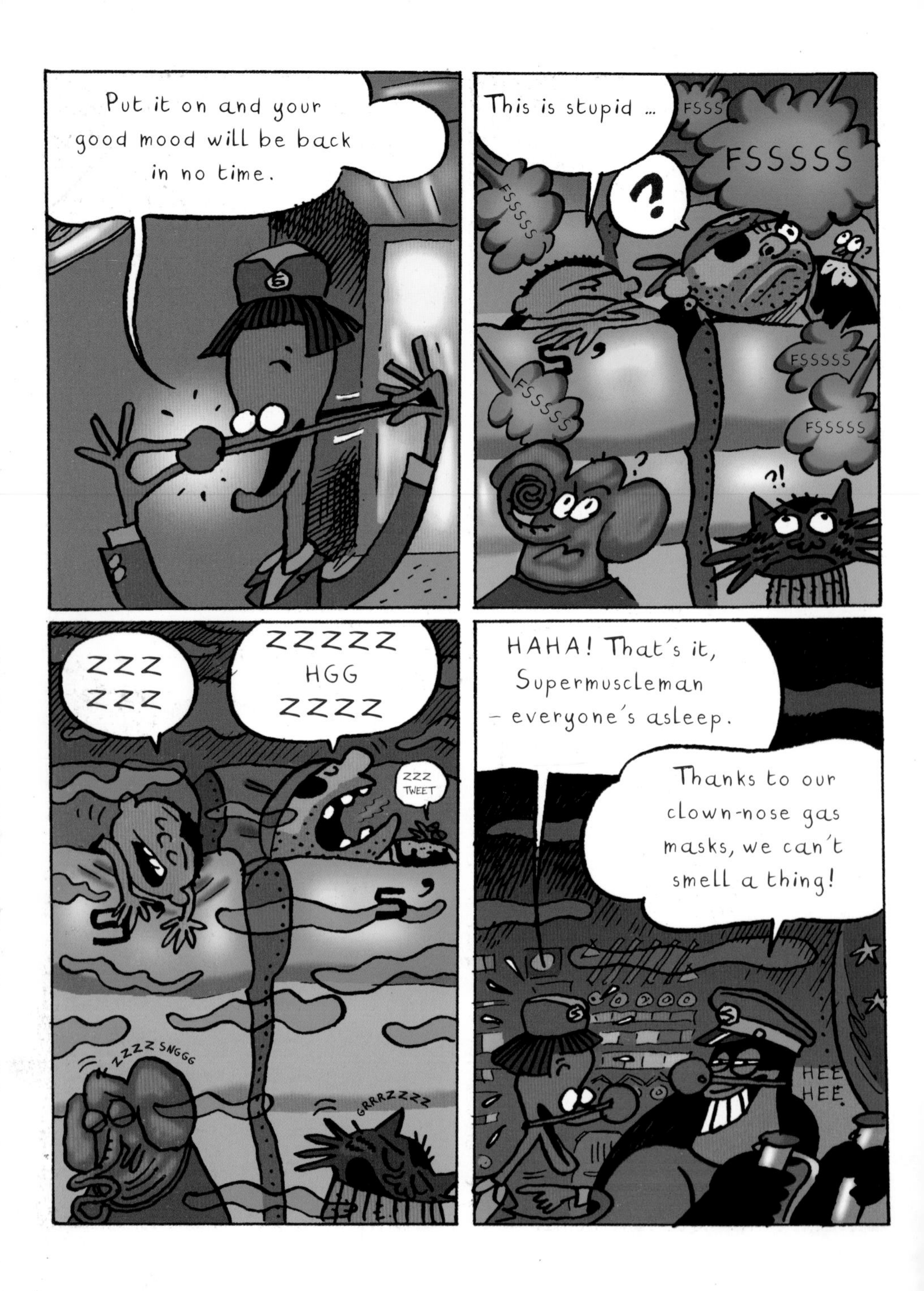
Put it on and your good mood will be back in no time.
This is stupid ...
FSSS
FSSSSS
?
FSSSSS
FSSSSS
FSSSSS
FSSSSS
?!
ZZZ ZZZ
ZZZZZ HGG ZZZZ
ZZZ TWEET
ZZZZ SNGGG
GRRRZZZZ
HAHA! That's it, Supermuscleman – everyone's asleep.
Thanks to our clown-nose gas masks, we can't smell a thing!
HEE HEE

Now I'll start the Pilot-o-Matic.
And we'll tie up that fatso Yellow Shoulder.
Let me try!
OH, dose scoudrels! Dey pud Ungle add by fredds to sleeb!
Peepee Room
If I open the bathroom porthole, the sleeping gas should clear out.
Hey, you! Pilot-o-Matic! Where are you taking us?
To the plane-tentiary.

Don't do that!
It's rotten there! Take us to our grandma's instead, and you can have some of her fig jam!
I can't, my course is set.
C'mon, be nice! There'll be plum pie, too! And fresh nougat!
Okay, cool, I'll change course!
Say, Doc Krok, are we turning around?
Yes. Something's not ri–
POW!
BAM!
OUCH!
OW!

Bravo, Pilot-o! When you made a U-turn, you knocked out those two creeps!
They fastened everyone to their seats but themselves!
Uncle! Uncle, wake up!
Hm?
Supermuscleman and Doc Krok tried to hijack us, but I turned the tables on them!
Nice, Sardine!
Now that's what I call tying up loose ends!
That'll teach them to try and hijack space pirates!
Mmf. Yawn!

Later, at Grandma's ...
Because Supermuscleman and Doc Krok tried putting everyone in jail, they don't get dinner.
It's great when an episode ends in a feast.
Yeah, they should all end like this!
gnaw gnaw
Have some more plum pie, Pilot-o. You earned it!
SNARFL
GULP
SLURP
The End

Crime and Space
Murder in Space!
Sa-Sardine! Help! I just saw a space ca-a sp-space ca ...
A space cadet? So what?
... A SPACE CADAVER!
That's a bit more troubling.
OLD BLACK JOE

People don't usually die in our stories. Are you sure it's a real corpse?
C'mon!
SAM SHO
Look – see?
Whoa! And he was stabbed, too!
His heart's not beating.
How about mine? I've never checked!
Let's go warn Uncle.
Darn! My ear can't reach my chest!

Soon ...
This is very serious, kids! If there's a victim in outer space, it must mean there's a murderer about.
Let's look for him!
Let's catch him!
HUCKLEBERRY
But where? Space is huge. Anyone could've done it and run away.
I have an idea! Look!
?
What's that?
A crime novel. It'll help us find the killer.
Crime and Space

I just finished reading it. It takes place on a rocket.
What's it about?
One night, in the rocket-ship library, an astronaut was found murdered.
The odd part was that the library door had been locked from the inside, and there was no other way out!
?
!
So they called the great space detective, Sherlock Rocket!

He solved the mystery. There was a secret trapdoor in the library, and the murderer was the astronauts' leader!
I get it!
You want to call Sherlock Rocket, too!
No, dummy! Sherlock Rocket's not real, he's a person in a book!
So what do we do, then?
Help me move the victim to the Huckleberry's library.
And then?
Then, we'll follow the book exactly as it's written. That way, we'll find the murderer in the end, too.

There. The victim's in place.
All that's left is to lock the room from the inside and leave.
Wait, no – silly me! Then we won't be able to leave!
WHAP!
That's true.
I'll stay in the library if we bring in the TV and get rid of the body.
Otherwise, it's kind of depressing.
Oh well. C'mon, we'll just lock it from outside.
Yeah. It's all the same in the end.
LUV ♥ ALWIN

What do we do now?
We keep our eyes peeled and wait.
For what?
The KILLER!
scrtch scrtch!
space Pirates
The murderer will revisit the scene of the crime. He'll enter through the secret trapdoor!
Alas, Sardine –
– I'm afraid our library doesn't have a secret trapdoor.
Darn! We'll have to build one!
Crime and Space
Why don't we just leave the door wide open? The murderer'll come and go normally, and we'll see him, since we're right here!
Not bad.
No sweat!
L'il Louie's right. Let's open the do –
KNOCK KNOCK
?

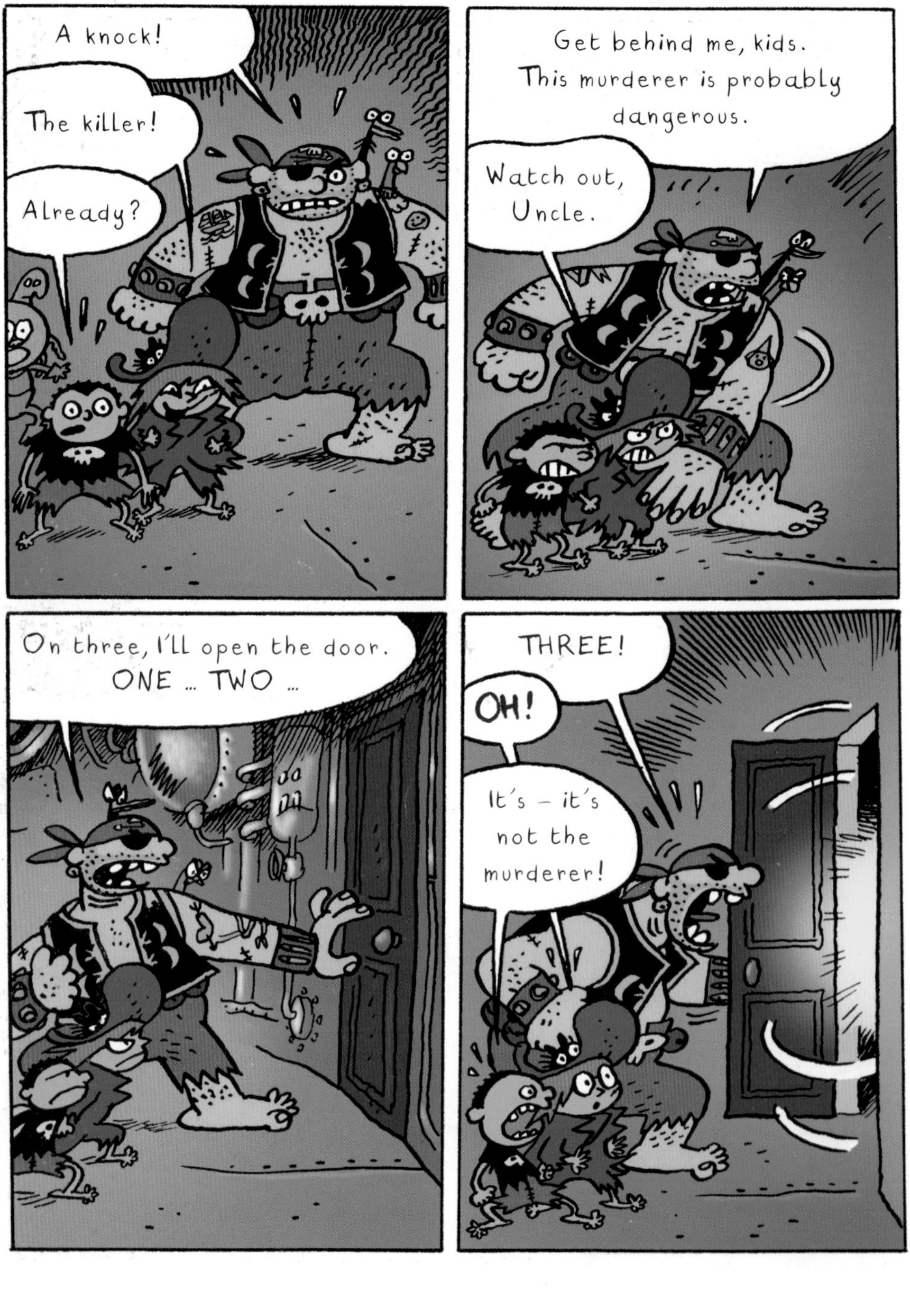

A knock!
The killer!
Already?
Get behind me, kids. This murderer is probably dangerous.
Watch out, Uncle.
On three, I'll open the door. ONE ... TWO ...
THREE!
OH!
It's – it's not the murderer!

It's the victim!
Can someone tell me what I'm doing here?
coo chi coo chi coo
We found you floating in space, sir. You were – uh ... dead.
Dead? I wasn't dead, I was just resting!
But you had a knife in your –
What of it? That's how we carry knives where I'm from.
POP!
And your heart wasn't beating.
That's because you weren't listening in the right place. My people's hearts are in their feet. Wanna feel?
BOOM
BOOM
POP!

But why were you going around with a knife?
Haven't you guessed? It's for my job. I'm a killer.
There you go! We solved the mystery. The victim was the murderer.
Nifty!
BLACK ELK SPEAKS
Later.
Since no one ever dies in this comic, I'll have to ply my trade elsewhere.
Yep, sorry.
Try TV!
HUCKLEBERRY
Hey Sardine, can you listen and tell me if my heart's beating?
dweeb
The End

Sardine and the Light Rail
What's a wormhole, Uncle?
It's a shortcut through space and time.
What's inside?
The Light Rail.
TIMES SQUARED
Star Map

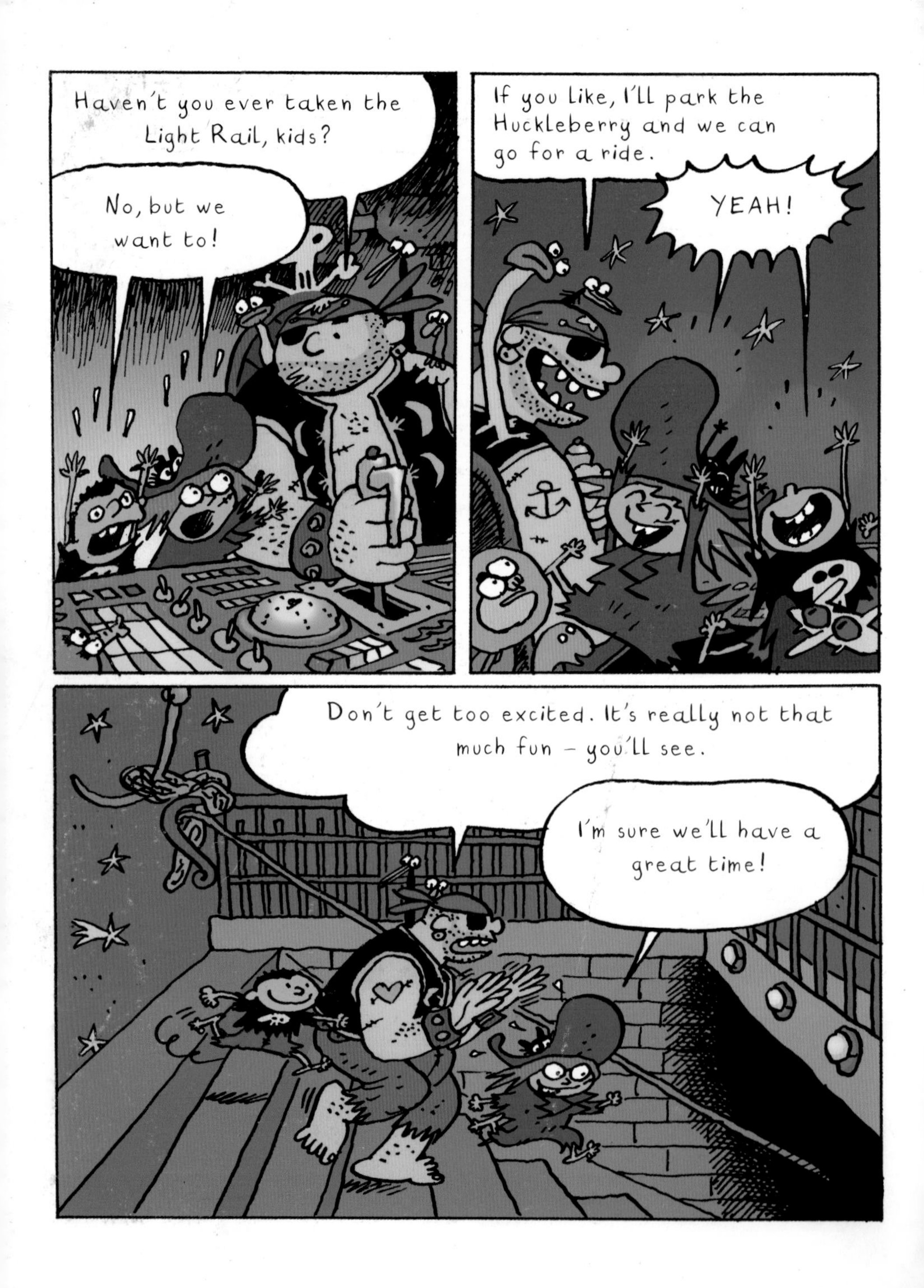
Haven't you ever taken the Light Rail, kids?
No, but we want to!
If you like, I'll park the Huckleberry and we can go for a ride.
YEAH!
Don't get too excited. It's really not that much fun – you'll see.
I'm sure we'll have a great time!

At the bottom of the wormhole, on the Light Rail platform.
What a crowd!
It's rush hour; all the space monsters are getting off work.
It smells funny.
There's the Light Rail!
eeeeeeeeeeeEEEE
Where to, Uncle?
Hop in, kids.
PARADISE DEMONS

Wherever we want. The Light Rail connects all the wormholes in space.
City Hole
Fourth Dimension Street
Times Squared
Gravity Central
Relativity Avenue
Warp Boulevard
Hey! Did you see this sign?
NO
Talking or Laughing
On Board
Violators Will Be
FINED!
Everyone's so quiet and gloomy in here, it's like they've been buried alive.
We'll fix that. EVENING, LADIES AND GENTS!

I'M CAPTAIN YELLOW SHOULDER, SPACE PIRATE! MY TWO KIDS AND I WOULD LIKE TO JOKE AND TALK AND ENTERTAIN YOU A LITTLE!
SILENCE, SCOUNDREL!
CHIEF
What are those two dimwits doing on the Light Rail?
Supermuscleman and Doc Krok!
We're the conductors! We make sure no one has a good time!
Yeah!
CHIEF
CHIEF JR.

In accordance with Wormhole Security measures, we're arresting you!
HANDS UP!
CHIEF
PUNCH
CHIEF JR.
PUNCH
What'll we do, Sardine? Get off at the next stop?
No, I've got a plan.
Hey, Supermuscleman! What do you do with a laughing sunbeam?
?
?
SILENCE, SARDINE! Talking is forbidden!
Leave it be, Doc Krok. I know the answer.
PUNCH
CHIEF
CHIEF JR.
PUNCH

You should fine it for laughing, Sardine. And that's the last riddle you'll ever tell.
Well said!
CHIEF
Not at all! You should put it in a prism!
HAHAHA
I get it!
slap
slap
Put it in a PRISM!
That's a good one!
HA HA

HEE HEE HEE
OH OH OH
haw haw
HA HA
HO HO HO!
har har
HEH HEH
HEE HEE HEE
HAHA
HOO H
ah ah ah
HO HO
QUIET! LAUGHING IS FORBIDDEN!
HAHA HEE
HAHA
HOHO
FINES FOR EVERYONE!
HA HA HA HA HA HA
HA HA
HAHAHA
PUNCH
PUNCH
CHIEF
CHIEF JR.
PUNCH
Uncle! The Light Rail's stopped!
Now or never, kids! Follow me!
PIPA

We'll go out one door ...
... and through another!
Prepare to be boarded!
After a brief but fierce struggle ...
HOORAY!
ATTENTION, PASSENGERS! We proclaim the right to talk and laugh on the Light Rail!
And other places too!
NO

As for Supermuscleman and Doc Krok, it looks like the last laugh's on them!
POW
ouch
OW
Later ...
I told you we'd have a good time on the Light Rail.
HAHAHA!
I get it! The last laugh's on them!
TIMES SQUARED
Star Map
The End
The End, The End ... that's all you ever say!

The Dancing Star
Look at these children, Yellie! Always poorly dressed and up to no good!
They're happy like that, Mama.

I'm not saying they're unhappy. I'm saying they've been poorly raised. Especially Sardine.
Sardine's adorable.
She may be, but she's a real tomboy, and since you're not doing anything to change that, I've decided to take action.
Oh no.
SUBJECT TO CHANGE
I've signed her up for dance lessons with you, me, Little Louie, and the others. It'll do us good.
WHAT?
Off we go! Class starts in an hour, and Madame Kruchalova won't be kept waiting.
But Mom ...

Later.
Where are we, Uncle?
Sadly, Sardine, you'll know soon enough.
DING DONG
LA KRUCHALOVA
DANCNG STAR
And you are?
I'm Grandma, and these are my kids. We've come for ballet lessons.
Go to the changing room for boys' and girls' outfits. Then, to work!
LA KRUCHALOVA
NG STAR

Soon ...
Well? Ready?
We're ready, Madame Kruchalova.
I still don't get what we're doing here, Uncle.
Me neither.
Together we shall practice the beautiful ballet, Swan Planet. But first, warm up!
Place your foot on the bar like this, and keep your back very straight.
KRACK

BRUTE! What have you done!?
Yellie! Tell the lady you're sorry!
I'm – uh – sorry, I've got – clumsy feet.
Don't touch ANYTHING! I shall now show you how it's done. Music, Master Igor Tovarisch!
SNAP!
Da.
The dance requires lightness.
OH!
AH!

Control.
Pretty!
Beautiful!
Harmony.
Splendid!
Magnificent!
In short, a lot of work.
Well, duh.
Of course.
Gotta work!
clap clap
clap clap
clap clap
clap clap
DING DONG
Start your exercises while I answer the door.

And you are?
Limbs up, ballerina! You're coming with me.
What do you want with me?
Ever hear of Supermuscleman? He's my boss, and it's his birthday soon.
I'm going to put on a variety show to celebrate. I'll sing while you and your students dance behind me. We'll be Doc Krok and the Krockettes!
Horrrrible! Atrocious vulgarity!

Now that you're not going any-where, I'll go get your troupe.
HANDS UP!
You're surrounded!
?!
Hey, look! It's Doc Krok!
Did you come to dance, Doc?
Can I teach him, Uncle?
AAAAAAAAAAH!
Watch closely, Madame Kruchalova!
?

Fisticuffs require finesse ...
THWACK!
OUCH!
... A light touch ...
... Flexibility ...
WHAM
WHAM
WHAM
WHAM
WHAM
In short, it's an art.
Splendid!

You have saved my honor. How can I ever thank you?
HMPH! Not easy!
Please – dance for us.
Bravo, Madame Kruchalova! You're marvelous!
clap clap clap clap
Li'l Louie, why are you dressed like a girl?
I'm not! This had a guy's name on it.
No, silly! Leo Tard isn't a name!
The End

The Brain of Professor Mush
Unfortunately, we will not be showing this week's "Mysteries of the Universe," hosted by the great scientist, Professor Mush.
TELE ROLL
Oh, nuts!
We waited all week!
BODY BY WINE

Professor Mush, the man who knows it all, has become a total moron. In the words of his assistant:
TELEROLL
A few days ago, the Professor had a bad cold. *Sniff* And last night, tragedy struck: *Sniff* he sneezed his brains out!
A-da-da.
Superspecialized Research Laboratory
His brain came out his right nostril and vanished into space! *Sniff* Ever since then, he's been speaking gibberish.
Timisheen La poo poo
In the name of science, *Sniff* I beg you: if you find the Professor's brain, please bring it back!
Aboglooboo Aboglooba
Research
Laborator

Let that be a lesson, kids: never sneeze too hard.
Uncle, can we help find his brain?
Yeah! That way there'll be a new episode next week!
LE ROLL
Where would you go if you were really smart, Uncle?
Hm. I've never asked myself that.
We could go looking in Geometric Space. I've heard smart types hang out there.
Let's go!

Meanwhile ...
We must find Professor Mush's brain before anyone else gets to it, Supermuscleman.
FLAP FLAP
FLAP FLAP
What for, Doc Krok?
Because then I'll operate on you and stick it in your head.
I've already got a brain in my head!
I'll put it in right beside yours. You've got room for two. That way, your already exceptional intelligence will be utterly astounding.
And that won't tire me out?
Not at all, Supermuscleman. It'll make life easier. For me too.
Well, okay then.
FLAP FLAP
FLAP FLAP

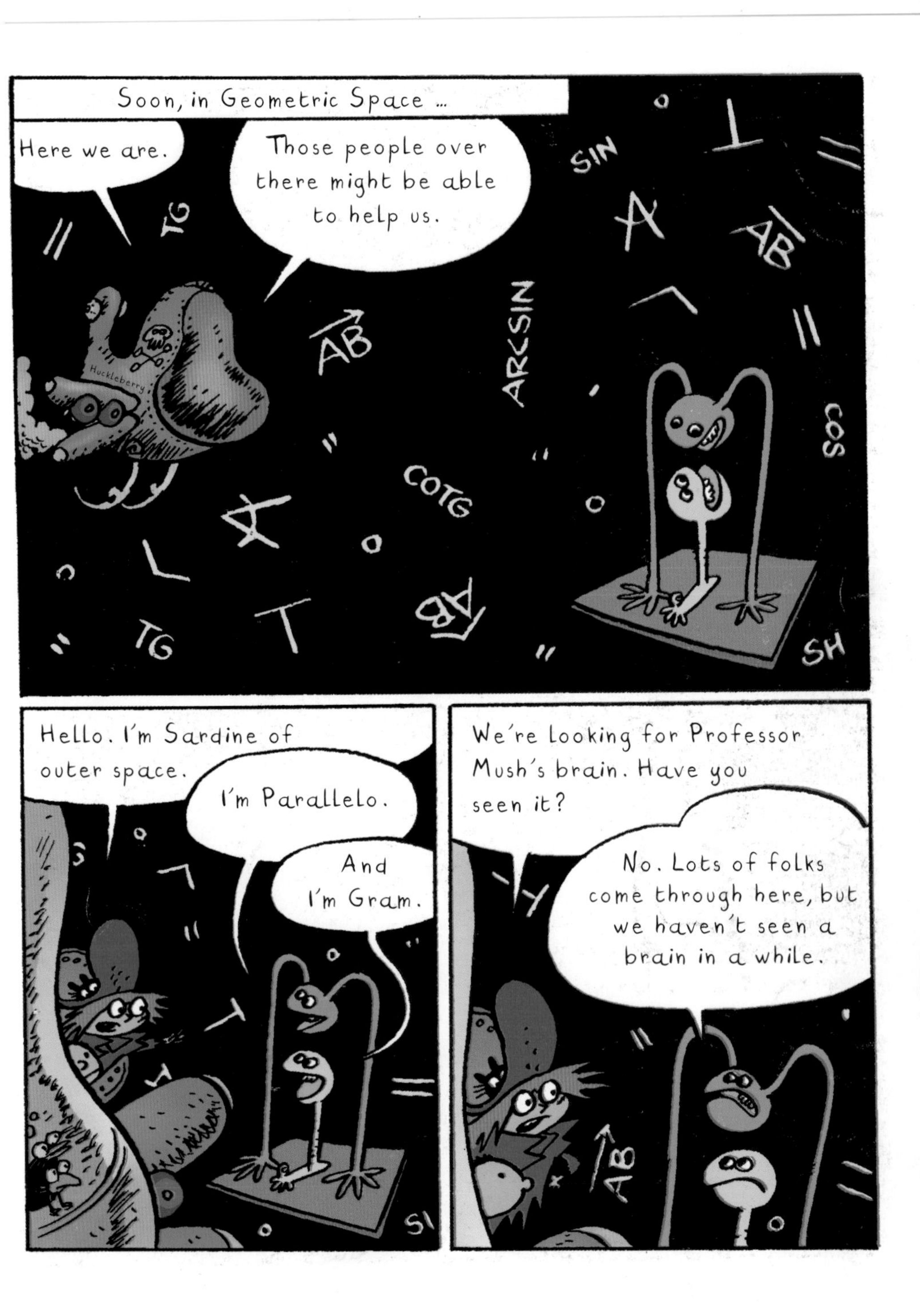
Soon, in Geometric Space ...
Here we are.
Those people over there might be able to help us.
Huckleberry
Hello. I'm Sardine of outer space.
I'm Parallelo.
And I'm Gram.
We're looking for Professor Mush's brain. Have you seen it?
No. Lots of folks come through here, but we haven't seen a brain in a while.

Follow us. We'll take you to The Circle.
There's a guy there who knows everything about everything.
Thanks!
Parallelo and Gram are cool.
Soon ...
THE CIRCLE
A Restaround
Tel.:
Pi. 31416
Sardine, may I present The Pro.
Hello, mister.
Hey, kid.
We're looking for Professor Mush's brain.
Oh yeah, guy that sneezed too hard. I hoid about it.

Sorry – ain't seen nothin'.
WHOA! Sardine, look!
Supermuscleman and Doc Krok!
Let's hide!
We've come for the brain of Mush!
Hands up and hand it over!
AB
COS
If those crooks find the brain before we do, it's all over!
Uncle, I've got an idea!

I'll peel off this old chewing gum someone stuck under the table.
– and make a big sticky ball.
Yuck!
pat
paff
pluff
Psst! Hey! Mister Pro! Can you give this to them?
Heh! I get it, kid!
Here's whatcher lookin' fer, Supermuscleguy.
What is that? It looks like a big ball of ch –
THE BRAIN! Give it over!

Quick! To the Space-Bat! I'm going to operate!
What if I just stuck it on my forehead, Doc? Wouldn't that be enough?
Later, on board the Huckleberry ...
– so Supermuscleman and Doc Krok left with this gooey wad of chewing gum they thought was Professor Mush's brain!
HAHAHAHAHA!
HAHAHA
The sad part is, we still don't know where the real brain is.
Yes you do!!
I'm right here!
?

Well, I'll be!
What are you doing on the Huckleberry, Profess – er – Professor Brain?
Surprised, huh? You thought you'd find me performing calculations in Geometric Space, perhaps? Not a chance!
When an intelligent brain escapes, it only has one thought: having fun with kids.
We might not know all the mysteries of the universe, true –
– but we sure know how to have a good time!
The End

scritch scratch
The Elector Detector
Supermuscleman, I need your help for our next poster campaign.
You wanna take my photo, Doc Krok?
SM

No, I need to make a cast. Stand under that shower-head.
With my clothes on?
Yes, yes. Stay as you are.
SPLOOSH!
?
There – don't move! I'll stick two little straws in your nostrils so you can breathe.
?
W!
I told you not to move!

Later.
Supermuscleman, I shall now unveil my invention before your, er – stunned eyes.
You hurt me, Doc Krok.
SUPERMUSCLE MAN
Ta-daa! A la kazam!
SUPERMUSCLE MAN
PRESIDENT
Since you can't see the poster, I'll describe it to you. It shows you in 3D, moving and talking!

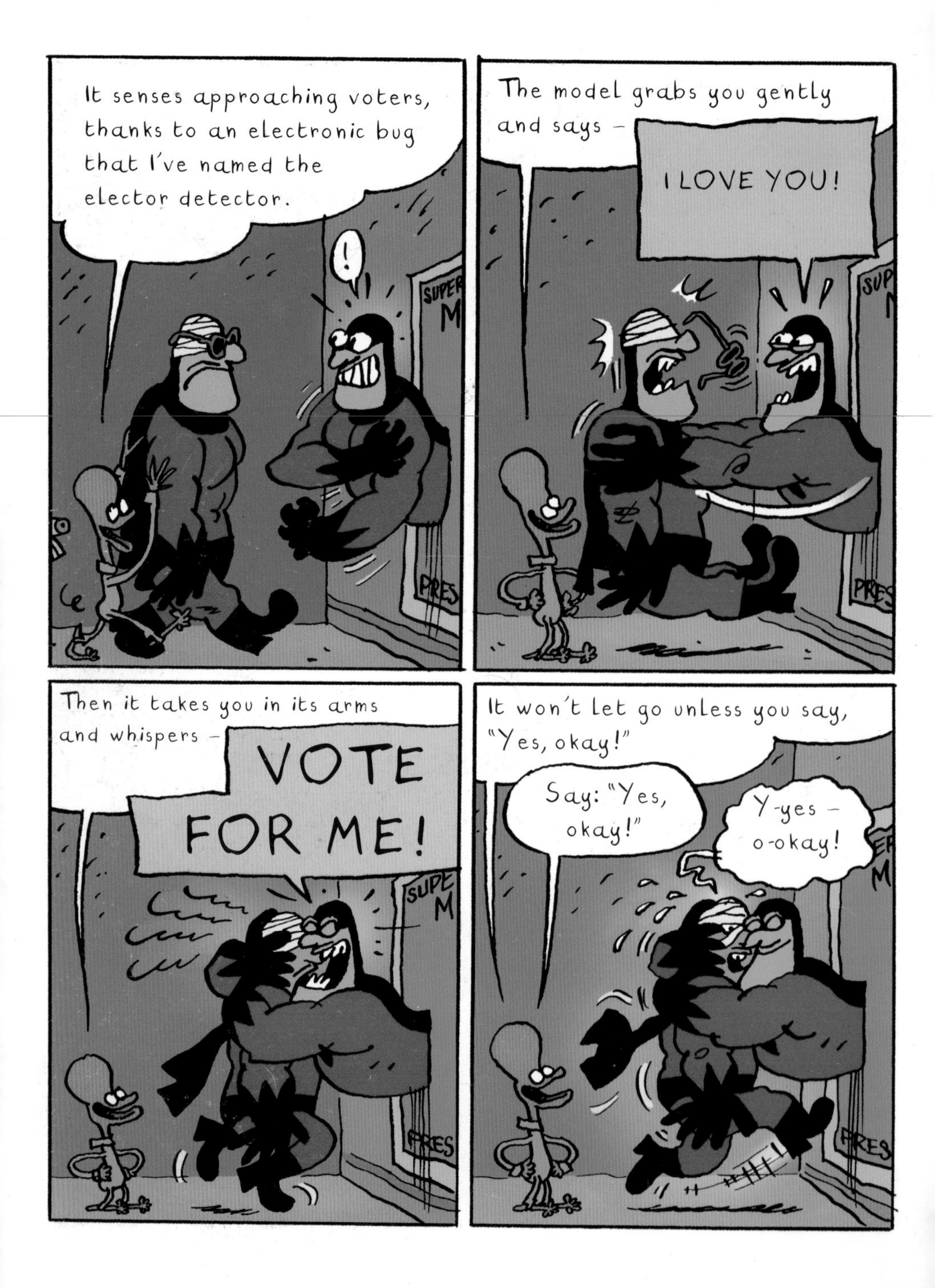
It senses approaching voters, thanks to an electronic bug that I've named the elector detector.
!
SUPER M
PRES
The model grabs you gently and says –
I LOVE YOU!
Then it takes you in its arms and whispers –
VOTE FOR ME!
It won't let go unless you say, "Yes, okay!"
Say: "Yes, okay!"
Y-yes – o-okay!

You've just seen what this poster does to your supporters. Now let's see what it does to your enemies!
Y-yes – o-okay ...
SUPER
M
PRES
I've made a Sardine doll to place in front of it.
SUPERMUS
MAN
PRESIDE
Watch: first, it seizes her.
IT'S JUST US NOW, SARDINE!
?
MA
PRES
Then it tears her apart.
TAKE THAT! AND THAT!
THAT'LL TEACH YOU!
Heh heh!
THWACK!
RRIP!
CRUNCH!
PRES

Well, Supermuscleman? What do you think of my poster?
Very effective, Doc Krok.
I made another, more traditional one – look.
GRRR
UMPF
ZNORT
WANTED
SARDINE OF OUTER SPACE
REWARD: A DREAM VACATION FOR TWO ON A TROPICAL ISLAND (PLANE, 4-STAR ✱✱✱✱ HOTEL, & MEALS INCLUDED)
Oh yes, very good!
Come, Supermuscleman. We'll put them up right next to each other throughout the cosmos.
The one with me on it should really stick out. It could almost even cover the other one.
flap
flap
flap

The next day, on a street in space.
Oh wow! Look, Uncle, L'il Louie! There's a price on my head! How cool is that?!
I want a price on my head too!
WANTED
SARDINE OF OUTER SPACE
REWARD: FULLY EQUIPPED KITCHEN WITH CONVECTION OVEN, DISHWASHER, AND OVERSIZE FREEZER
Here's what I think of that rag!
No, Uncle! Don't tear it up! It'd make a great poster for our room!
SNATCH
krump! krump!
Too late, it's all wrinkled.
Don't toss it on the street, at least. Littering's a dirty habit.
HEY! LOOK!

Supermuscleman's coming out of the wall!
What's this?
SUPERMUSCLE MAN
PRESIDENT
BICEPS
Let's get closer.
IT'S JUST US NOW, SARDINE!
Wha-?!
SUPERMUSCLE MAN
DENT
TAKE THA-
BOING!
SU MUSCLE AN
ZZZZNN
PRESIDEN
?

SUPERMUSCLE MAN
OW!
CRACK
WHAM
WHOOF
That's not Supermuscleman! That's a robot!
Watch out, Sardine! Something fell on top of your hat!
scritch scratch
rub rub
Your cat's scratching itself.
I see what it is!
scritch scratch
An electronic bug!
Let's see what it has to say.

It says it's an elector detector and Sardine trap invented by Doc Krok.
Give it here.
That's how I treat Doc Krok's inventions!
Heh heh!
S.TOMP!
Let's go see if there are other robots like that one. With my cat attracting pesky electronic bugs, we can disable them.
Look, Sardine! I found a trash bin for the crumpled poster. Now the streets'll stay clean!
SUPERMUSCLE MAN
The End

My Cousin Manga
My cousin Manga's coming to spend a few days with us. We're waiting for her at the space station.
There's her train now!
How will we recognize Cousin Manga? We've never seen her before!
NEWSPAPERS
WORRY WARTS
Feed me!
Feed me!
TICKET PUNCHER

I sent her our comics. She'll recognize us.
Right, good idea.
Being famous helps. We don't recognize people, but they recognize us.
Apparently, Cousin Manga's even more famous than we are.
More famous? Fat chance.
No, really, I swear.
She's got comics too. And she sells a thousand times as many!
MY EYE!
Besides, Uncle, look – we're not the only ones waiting for her.
Huh?

YAY MANGA
WELCOME MANGA
I LOVE MANGA
MANGA
Those are her fans.
?
They just haven't seen us yet. Just you wait, I'll show 'em.
Hey, pals, recognize me? It is I, Captain Yellow Shou–
IT'S HER!
WELCOME MANGA
I LOVE MANGA
MANGA

You okay, Uncle?
What BRATS! They ran right over me!
Hey there! Sardine! Yellow Shoulder! L'il Louis!
An auto!
A photo!
Auto-graph, Miss Manga?
One photo, please!
Autograph! Please!
SWOOOOSH!
My photo!
What the-
WHEE!

HEY THERE, COUSINS!
BAMM!
Uh ... hey, cousin.
You can really jump!
And you have very pretty eyes.
HA HA! I'm so happy to meet you! How are you?!
Good, good.
Not bad.
MANGA
WELCO MANG
MANGA
Shall we go? There are too many fans.
It's true, they're pretty annoying.
C'mon, cousin. We're parked over here.
EXIT

Soon.
Well, Cousin Manga? How do you like our little ship?
HA HA! Very nice! Very pretty! But –
But?
It's a little old, no? Don't you think?
Yeah, that's true.
It's not super-new, but it works well.
Look! This is a photo of my spaceship, the Walter.
WOW!
Amazing!

Uncle! Couldn't we get a ship like that for a change?
Of course not! It's much too expensive!
You could borrow the money from Grandma!
SPONSOR
GLOVE BOX
What's more, two rowdy kids like you would wear it out in a flash.
No we wouldn't!
We'd be careful!
Who's that guy up there?
Him? That's Supermuscleman, the evil dictator.
Our sworn enemy.

He's not very terrifying.
That's because he looks dumb. But he's really dangerous.
This is my enemy. He's called Domoarigatogozaimashita!
Yikes!
Freaky!
He's really scary!
How do you fight him, cousin?
Easy!
I've got tons of the latest gadgets!
Naturally!
Of course!

I'm having a great time! It's a nice change of pace from my normal life.
Say, cousin, I just thought of something ...
burp
koff koff
krunk
What if we switched places for a few days? We'd lend you our ship, our universe, and our villains, and you'd lend us yours.
What a great idea!
And afterward we'd meet up and swap stories.
YEAH! I'll take care of Supermuscleman – just wait!
Hee Hee Hee
WHAM WHAM WHAM WHAM

But before you visit my universe, I have to give you a little makeover.
Cool! Disguises!
Uh - do we really have to?
MAKEUP KIT
ARGO
Later.
There! You're all set!
Hey, Sardine. I don't think I mind anymore that we sell fewer comics - All I want is my old look back.
Oh c'mon, just give it a shot.
And we have pretty eyes now, see?
KAWASAKI CITY MUSEUM
The End

New York & London

Published by First Second
First Second is an imprint of Roaring Brook Press, a division of
Holtzbrinck Publishing Holdings Limited Partnership
175 Fifth Avenue, New York, NY 10010

Distributed in Canada by H. B. Fenn and Company Ltd.
Distributed in the United Kingdom by Macmillan Children's Books,
a division of Pan Macmillan.

Originally published in France in 2007 under the title
Sardine de l'espace 6: La cousine Manga by Dargaud.
www.dargaud.com

Design by Nicole Concepción and Danica Novgorodoff

Cataloging-in-Publication Data is on file at the Library of Congress.

ISBN-13: 978-1-59643-380-9
ISBN-10: 1-59643-380-9

First Second books are available for special promotions and premiums.
For details, contact: Director of Special Markets, Holtzbrinck Publishers.

First Edition June 2008
Printed in China

1 3 5 7 9 10 8 6 4 2

Some fine offerings from First Second for young readers of graphic novels...

And lots more to discover at

www.firstsecondbooks.com

If you enjoy Sardine's adventures,
please tell a friend!

MANGA
MANGA